Praise for the *Kingdom of Silk* series:

'A truly beautiful story of loss, hope, strength and love...unforgettable.' Jane Sandell, *The Scotsman*

'Poignant and lovely. Millard has that rare gift of making you feel in a few pages that you've known these characters, and this place, always.'
Daniel Hahn, *Independent on Sunday*

'Rarely has a series of books had such an effect on me. Never have I felt such yearning to be part of a fictional family. Never have I cried both of sorrow and elation as much as I have with every single book in this series. It really is a magnificent series.'
Mélanie McGilloway, *Library Mice*

'If you haven't heard of the *Kingdom of Silk* books then it's high time you discovered them.'
Alison Potter, *Junior Magazine*

'A beautifully crafted story... Glenda Millard has a genius for letting the plot unfold.'
Ann Lazim, *Centre for Literacy in Primary Education*

'A special, lyrical and lovely story... It will surely touch your heart.' *Berlie Doherty*

'Guarante   ...:l.. '

Lancashire

The *Kingdom of Silk* series:

The Naming of Tishkin Silk

Layla Queen of Hearts

Perry Angel's Suitcase

All the Colours of Paradise

Plum Puddings and Paper Moons

The Tender Moments of Saffron Silk

Nell's Festival of Crisp Winter Glories

The Tender Moments of SAFFRON SILK

by Glenda Millard
Illustrated by Stephen Michael King

For Hepsey — G.M.
For David and Melissa — S.M.K.

Contents

1. A Daddy and His Daughter *1*

2. Bluebirds and Firebirds *15*

3. Saffron's Other Brother *28*

4. Elephant Clouds and Afternoon Tea *35*

5. Tools for Truth *43*

6. Sir Attenborough and the Velvet Worms *51*

7. Different Ways of Looking *60*

8. The Loud Silence of Saffron Silk *67*

9. Saint Lucy's Cats *75*

10. Farewell to Little Petal *84*

11. Double Happiness *93*

12. Science and Technology
vs Tender Moments *103*

13. An Invitation *112*

1. A Daddy and His Daughter

'I saw the angel in the marble and carved until I set him free.'

The shed on which these words were chalked belonged to Ben Silk. Ben often saw angels but none of them were made of marble. They were live and loud with cherry-tart cheeks and bare feet, wearing daisy-chain halos on their tumbling hair and wings made of wire coathangers and chicken

1

feathers. Some days they danced amongst the tussocky grass where new lambs play. On others they might wander between the soft blue folds of the hills or sleep in the sun on bales of sweet yellow straw, their wings tethered to the clothesline like cloudlets. These were the children of the Kingdom of Silk.

The words on the wall of Ben's shed belonged to a famous painter and sculptor called Michelangelo, who lived many hundreds of years ago. Ben was not a famous painter or sculptor; he was father of the sometimes-winged children, drove a beaten-up old Bedford truck and collected things other people had no use for. He was excellent at playing harmonica, cotton-reel knitting, and building tree houses and many other useful things. His shed was cluttered with items such as planks from disused jetties, railings from rickety bridges, decaying fenceposts from forsaken farms, unlabelled tins half-filled with paint, bent bicycle wheels, ropes and pulleys, inside-out umbrellas, wire coathangers and chicken feathers in hessian sacks.

It was Saffron, the fifth of Ben and Annie Silk's daughters, who wrote Michelangelo's words on the wall of her daddy's shed. Saffron was well informed about historical figures such as Michelangelo, Joan of Arc and Cleopatra. She had also studied the myths and legends of Greek and Roman gods and goddesses. But one of the most interesting living people Saffron knew was her daddy, because of his ability to see things that other people could not. Extraordinary and unexpected things like mermaidenly ladies in driftwood branches, wild horses rearing from red gum fenceposts, wings in wire coathangers and angels in the cabbage patch.

The gift of seeing, like all special talents, takes practice and practice takes time. Ben often practised on his Seat of Wisdom, which had once been a dentist's chair. He positioned his seat directly under a skylight in the roof of his shed so he could see birds flying and clouds passing and so he would know he'd been there too long if he could see the moon and stars.

Sometimes while he was wondering how best to show other people what he could see, Ben knitted tea cosies or odd socks. On other occasions he watched dust fairies floating in streams of light and, from time to time, he pulled a lever and lowered the chair just enough so he could draw finger pictures in the sawdust on the floor. Now and then he just sat and thought. Thinking deeply was encouraged at the Kingdom of Silk. At first glance it would be easy to conclude that Ben was wasting time, but Saffron knew better. She believed wholeheartedly that her daddy would one day be as famous as Michelangelo and would go down in history as the Seer of Cameron's Creek.

Seeing what other people could not wasn't the only thing Ben did when he sat in his Seat of Wisdom. It was there, long before Saffron was born, that he dreamt of making Naming Day Books for his children and of a ceremony at which they would be presented. In the weeks and months before each ceremony, Ben spent hours sorting through his collection of useful pieces of wood. From these he would carve covers for the books to protect the precious memories of his children's lives; their minutes, hours, days and years.

When Ben shared his dream with Annie, she made paper to cushion the words she would write for each of her babies. Pages and pages she made from torn wallpaper scraped from old walls.

Each sheet was embedded with secrets from past inhabitants of their house on the hill. Each leaf was scented with smoke from fires that once warmed other people's children. There were enough pages to hold everything Annie knew about the babies who had grown in the quiet dark inside her; the moments before, during and after their births on the bed that Ben made and the wonderful celebrations of their Naming Days. But, wisely, Annie always made more pages than she knew how to fill. Empty pages for moments yet to be lived. Words yet to be spoken on days yet to dawn. For she knew that every baby held mysteries only time would reveal.

Of the seven Naming Day Books, only one was complete. It was the one made for Tishkin, the youngest of the Silk sisters. For time is a gift and Tishkin's time with her family was as brief as the spring daisies that yellowed the hills of Cameron's Creek. The perfect amount of time it took for her family to fall in love with her. Tishkin comes to them still, in the wind, the rain and the sun, and in the rustling of leaves they hear her name. But although she is for always and forever at the heart

of the Kingdom of Silk, she leaves no footprints in the garden. The other books belong to Tishkin's brother, Griffin, and to her sisters, the Rainbow Girls: Scarlet, Indigo, Violet, Amber and Saffron.

When Perry arrived at the Kingdom of Silk, he already had a name. The golden letters on the suitcase he brought with him stood for Perry Maxwell, God's Dearest Angel. He was called Perry Angel for short. There was no need for a Naming Day celebration. But the Silk family were fond of merrymaking, ritual and ceremony, so when Griffin's best friend, Layla, suggested a Day of Cake and Thankfulness to welcome Perry to his new home, they readily agreed.

Days after Saffron's birth, Ben held her in his arms while he sat on his Seat of Wisdom as he had done with each of her four older sisters. They gazed at one another in the soft, sawdusty silence. Ben turned his small and precious child this way and that under the single yellow light bulb. He gazed at her starfish fingers, seashell ears, pearly nails and rockpool eyes. He watched her salty lashes sweep slowly open and shut like sea anemones and tried to imagine what sort of person his tiny girl might grow up to be.

You might think that Ben, Seer of Cameron's Creek, would have unravelled the mystery of babies, at least by the time his fifth daughter was born. But Ben had learnt that every baby is unique, and even after a year had passed it seemed there was more that Ben and the rest of the Silk family did *not* know about the newcomer than they did.

On the day of her naming ceremony, Saffron was still buttercup fresh, spring lamb new, a little mystery to them all. Ben raised his face to the sky and declared to the universe:

*'All we know about our fifth daughter is that
her hair is more lovely than marigolds.
All we know is
she is more rare and more precious
than the costliest spice.
All we know is
she is more beautiful to us than Aurora,
goddess of the dawn.
And for all that we know
we name this small and precious mystery
Saffron Silk.'*

After Ben had finished speaking, Annie placed a tiny circlet of white flowers and yellow ribbons on Saffron's head. Ben's words, and everything else that happened on Saffron's Naming Day, were recorded in her book. The wreath was dried and framed and hung on the wall above Saffron's bed. Annie painted its likeness in Saffron's Naming Day Book along with the following caption:

The flowers in this garland are freesias. They were grown from bulbs that Nell Silk was given by a stranger on her wedding day. The bulbs were transplanted from Nell's city garden to the Kingdom of Silk when she came with her son, Ben, and his wife, Annie, to live here. In the lore of flowers, the freesia represents innocence. The yellow ribbon signifies hope, happiness and kindness.

There are photographs of Saffron wearing a long white dress embroidered with buttercups and love by her wise and wonderful grandmother, Nell. Faded snapshots show her sisters playing in the sappy spring grass, trying to catch apple blossom in butterfly nets. In others, Amber and Barney Blacksheep watch curiously from the comfort of the old wicker pram in the shade of the Cox's Orange Pippin tree. Barney, an orphaned lamb, wears an organza bonnet and a knitted pink vest sprigged with ribbon rosebuds. If you look carefully at some of the photographs you will see that Amber is feeding Barney Blacksheep sugar-coated aniseed rings from Nell's handbag.

In Saffron's favourite photograph, she is cradled in Nell's arms. Her daddy has just finished reading his declaration and her mama is placing the garland of flowers on her marigold curls. The three people she loves most in the world are all looking at her with love and wishfulness in their eyes. It was probably one of the first tender moments in Saffron's life.

Not many people expect the world's leading authority on tender moments to be a small white-haired woman who doesn't drive a car or know how to operate a computer and who has no

ambition to learn how to. Nell Silk never attended a university because they do not offer courses in subjects such as the observation of tender moments. There is no technology, no textbook, no diagram or formula with clear instruction on how to identify and preserve them, pressed like forget-me-nots, between the pages of one's life. It is a hand-me-down skill usually passed on by wise and wonderful grandpeople to their children and grandchildren.

Some of these wise people live in mud huts or in homes made of ice or even in holes in the ground, and some live in palaces with golden taps and crystal chandeliers and heated toilet seats. Some wear diamonds in their teeth, some wear animal skins on their backs and some wear almost nothing at all. But each and every one will tell you that the skill of capturing a tender moment is the most wonderful thing they possess. It is more like magic than almost anything else in the universe, except perhaps reading hearts or books or seeing things that other people cannot. The observation of a tender moment brings unspeakable pleasure equally to the giver, the receiver and the observer.

According to Nell, life was a mixture of moments. Some are tiny and tender, like holding a just-hatched chick to your cheek. Others, like falling in love with a new baby, linger far longer. These moments can make your heart soar above the clouds for days or weeks or months, before they settle quietly, comfortably around you, like a hand-knitted scarf. Occasionally, there are heavy grey moments that make your heart ache for longer than you thought possible.

On the day of Saffron's naming, no one could tell what sort of moments would fill the pages of her book, but everyone hoped the tiny tender ones, those that make the soul tipsy with ordinary happiness, and the quiet comforting kind would far outweigh the others. This was their wish for her from the beginning, even before they learnt she had to go away.

2. Bluebirds and Firebirds

Saffron first saw the firebirds when she was at school. She wasn't alarmed, since she knew her daddy also saw things other people didn't. Besides, it was during her Joan of Arc phase, so she thought it possible the birds were a vision from the heavens. But she didn't tell anyone else about them.

Saffron, like her older sisters, had been home-schooled until Tishkin died. Then Annie became ill with sadness and had to go to a hospital far away in the city to learn how to be happy again. So the Rainbow Girls went by bus to a school in the next town and Griffin walked to Saint Benedict's School in Cameron's Creek.

Saffron was miserable at school. She missed her mama and Tishkin so badly that it hurt to breathe. She thought her heart was broken and that she had caught sadness sickness, so she begged her daddy and Nell to let her go to the hospital where Mama was, to learn how to be happy again. She buried her face in Nell's apron and felt her grandmother's body working; her warm heart squeezing, her quiet breath sighing in and out and her muscles tightening, trying to close down the tear-drop department.

One day soon after, when Saffron arrived home from school, Nell had a gift for her. It was a silver ring with a small enamelled bluebird on it. Nell said it was the bluebird of happiness and that it had been a gift from her Johnny when they were sweethearts.

'Johnny said that if anything ever happened to him he wanted me to look at this little bluebird and remember the happy times we'd shared. When Johnny and my girls, Katie and Ella, were killed in a car accident, I thought I'd never be happy again. Every time I looked at Johnny's ring, I'd cry. Even now, after all these years, when I look at the bluebird, my heart is squeezed. But Johnny was right, I learnt to remember the good times. It's all right to cry, Saffron, and it's all right to feel sad. It's normal and it helps the hurt in us heal. Annie needs special care but the rest of us just need each other. I promise that some day you'll be happy again. We all will, even your mama.'

Nell pushed the bluebird ring onto Saffron's thumb. It fitted perfectly.

'I'd like you to wear Johnny's ring. I can't fit it over my knuckles any more. When you look at it or feel it, I want you to remember how birds return in spring after the winter, to build their nests, to start again. If I hadn't lost Johnny and my girls, I might never have been lonely. I might never have welcomed a little boy called Ben into my home. I might never have known you. Happiness will come, sweetheart, happiness will come.'

Saffron wore the bluebird ring every day that Annie was away. Some days she cried and some days she did not. She still missed Tishkin and always would, but Nell was right: happiness, like the birds and like Annie, eventually returned to the family and to the Kingdom of Silk.

At school, Saffron learnt many things she didn't know. One of the strangest things was that other children's fathers did not knit tea-cosies or odd socks or even scarves. They didn't see things in lumps of wood either, or watch dust fairies dance in the light; and they didn't waltz under the stars with their wives. Other fathers had no Seat of Wisdom in their sheds, and other mothers did not sing to their goats to make the milk sweeter. In fact, most of them had no goats. Some children had never heard of Grandmother Magic and didn't understand what tender moments were. And the teachers didn't encourage cogitation. There was no time for thinking deeply. They wanted Saffron, like all the other students, to answer their questions quickly.

Saffron found school and all the people who went there strangely mysterious, as though they came from a different world. Even though she eventually got used to their strangeness, she wasn't sure they would understand if she told them about the firebirds.

By this time, Saffron was slightly less of a mystery to her family. They discovered she was excellent at pretending to be other people. This was something she inherited from Nell. Ever since Saffron could remember, Nell had played dress-up with her. Nell usually played the part of Fairy Grandmother, while Saffron almost always chose historical characters. Amongst her favourites were: Joan of Arc, also known as the Maid of Orleans; Hannibal, with his mighty army of elephants; Cleopatra, Queen of Egypt; and Anne of Green Gables. Joan, Hannibal and Cleopatra were real people. Strictly speaking, Anne was not. But when Saffron read the book, Anne seemed positively real to her. Anne was easier to become than the others because there was no need for horses, elephants, venomous snakes or burning at the stake, and also on account of her marigold hair.

Saffron even made costumes for the characters she liked to play. Once upon a time, it was Nell who made all the dressing-up clothes using a pedal-operated sewing machine. But now Saffron could pedal faster. She rarely ran the needle through her finger and, even when she did, she tried to be brave by reminding herself of the astonishing hardships her heroes and heroines had suffered. But even so, it is difficult to be courageous when you are in agony.

Uniforms were not compulsory at the school

the Rainbow Girls attended, so Saffron sometimes wore her costumes. Being called names by some of the other students didn't bother Saffron. There were worse things than being called a weirdo. At least weird was interesting, she thought.

During her Joan of Arc phase, Saffron wore her long white martyr's dress and hung a wooden cross whittled from kindling sticks around her neck on a bootlace. It was extremely difficult to look miserable all day but she managed until lunchtime, when some of the more curious students asked questions about her costume. Saffron explained how Joan saw visions that spoke to her and told her she had been chosen to help the rightful king of France. She led an army to drive out his enemies and, sadly, was put to death because of her beliefs, when she was only nineteen. It seemed to Saffron that this was a dreadful mistake, since many years later Joan was declared a saint.

The Maid of Orleans seemed to inspire a few of the other girls in Saffron's class. They took to wearing white dresses to school and asked Saffron if Ben would make them crosses. At home, Scarlet told everyone that Saffron had a cult following.

Saffron wasn't sure how many people it took to make a cult, but she was almost certain five wasn't enough. Then the drama teacher, Mr Chalmers, suggested the students stage a play about Joan for the Christmas concert. Saffron played the lead role. She and Nell made the costumes. Saffron wanted a real fire for the burning-at-the-stake scene, but Mr Chalmers said the school's insurance policy didn't cover deliberately lit fires. Even so, the play was a great success.

Joan of Arc had been laid to rest for months and Saffron was herself again. It was Sunday and she was dressed in a lumpy jumper knitted with Barney Blacksheep's wool by Nell. The air at the Kingdom of Silk was syrupy with the scent of sunburnt fruit. It was apple-pie season. Nell and Annie had made pastry on Saturday and Ben lit the outdoor oven early Sunday morning. Scarlet was at work at the Colour Patch Café. Everyone else, including Layla, was in the kitchen peeling and slicing apples, grinding cinnamon and cloves or rolling out sheets of buttery pastry. Nell had orders. Apple-pie orders. A list as long as her arm was stuck to the refrigerator. On top of the list Perry had written Jenkins' name with a fat red crayon so Nell couldn't possibly miss it.

Jenkins was Perry's grown-up friend. He was nearly eighty. His favourite things were driving the ride-on mower at the Cameron's Creek Cemetery, being Perry's personal assistant at school, and Nell. Nell thought Jenkins only liked her because of the plum puddings she made for him at Christmas, and the Barney Blacksheep socks she knitted him for winter. But Perry could tell that Jenkins loved

Nell for herself, just as *he* did.

Every year, Mr Canning from the orchard down the road donated apples. The Silk family, and anyone else who cared to help, made the pies and Ben cooked them in his oven. The apple-pie money always went to a worthy cause. This year it was going to people in the state of Queensland, whose homes had been washed away by floods. Perry's job was to cut shapes from the leftover scraps of pastry to use as decorations on top of the pies. He used a special leaf-shaped cutter and pressed lines into the pastry with a fork to make them look like the veins in real leaves.

Saffron was standing beside him, painting the tops of the pies with beaten egg then passing them to Layla, who sprinkled vanilla sugar over them. Saffron was very quiet but Perry didn't mind. He was quiet too, especially when he was concentrating hard on important things like putting veins in leaves. When almost all the pastry was used, Perry made two heart shapes. One for Miss Cherry, his teacher at school, and the other for Jenkins, because he loved them both. Pictures of hearts mean love. Scarlet had taught him that.

Perry was about to pass the hearts to Saffron,

when her pastry brush fell to the floor with a clatter. She grabbed at the table as though to stop herself falling and her face was as pale as butcher's paper.

Annie and Nell helped Saffron to her room, felt her forehead, fussed and asked too many questions.

'I need to lie down. Just leave me alone,' Saffron whispered, sinking onto the bed. At last they closed the door, blocking out light and sound and the smell of apples and spices. Saffron tore everything off, dumping it on the floor: jumper, jeans, underpants, the elastic that held her ropey red curls. Everything but her most precious possession, the enamelled bluebird ring. From the bottom of her wardrobe, she took the loose white martyr's tunic and slipped it over her head. Her skin hurt. Her eyes hurt. Everything hurt. She would rather have worn nothing at all, but she hoped Joan of Arc might give her courage for what lay ahead.

Saffron melted onto her bed and the lights came again. Little birds furiously beating fiery wings, darting in the darkness, burning a hot, tight halo around her head.

The birds had flown by Monday, but Saffron couldn't stand up without feeling dizzy. So she stayed in bed all day with the blinds pulled down and the lights switched off, a hot water bottle on her feet and an ice pack over her closed eyes. It wasn't the first time she'd felt this way. But the headaches seemed to be getting stronger, lasting longer and coming more often. It hurt to bend, to breathe, to be.

Saffron woke before sunrise on Tuesday, lifted the ice-pack, opened her eyes a crack and carefully turned her head sideways on the pillow. Annie was asleep in the wicker peacock chair beside her bed.

'Mama,' Saffron whispered and Annie woke in an instant. 'I think I'm better today.'

'You're sure?'

Saffron nodded, something she couldn't do when she wasn't well. Annie slipped into bed beside her and held her until Aurora trailed her golden robe across the sky.

'How do you know, Saffron?' Annie whispered, as though afraid words might wound her tender child. 'Is there something that tells you the headache is coming? Is there a sign?'

The Maid of Orleans saw visions. Some people said she was holy, others said she was mad. What would people say if she told them about the firebirds, Saffron wondered. Did other people see them too? How could she know without giving her secret away? Was she really as weird as the girls at school said she was? Saffron said nothing and rolled over into Annie's arms.

3. Saffron's Other Brother

By the time Saffron got out of bed, the house was quiet. Her sisters and Griffin were at school. Annie was in her studio painting and Ben had gone to collect some windows and doors from an old house that was being pulled down. He planned to use them to build an extension onto the house at the Kingdom of Silk. He left early so he could be back in time to take Saffron to her appointment with Doctor Larsson.

Barney Blacksheep was pretending to be invisible. He didn't usually come into the front room on a Tuesday, but Blue had been practising being a sheepdog, instead of just a regular dog. He was showing off to Saffron, who wasn't usually at home on Tuesdays. He'd been rounding up Barney, and Barney, being a very obliging sort of sheep, had allowed himself to be herded into the living room, where he was so exhausted from being chased all over the Kingdom of Silk that he lay down on the pink cabbage roses carpet and refused to budge. Saffron lay on the floor with her head on Barney's woolly middle, and Blue crouched in front of them, nose to paws, looking pleased with himself.

Perry Angel was there, too. He was home-schooled by Nell and Annie on Tuesdays and Thursdays. He liked Tuesdays. He called them *Choose-days* because on that day of the week he was allowed to decide what he wanted to learn. On this particular Choose-day, he was having a knitting lesson with Nell. Everyone at the Kingdom of Silk knew how to knit. Nell said knitting was a necessary survival skill. Ben liked knitting tea cosies, hot water bottle covers with cherry tassels, and odd socks. No one at the Kingdom of Silk ever wore matching socks. It took too much time to find their mates, and besides it was boring wearing the same colour or pattern on both feet. So Ben kept up a steady supply of odd socks. Griffin liked cotton-reel knitting best. He wanted to make metres and metres of long woollen tubes, like knitted spaghetti, using small leftover pieces of wool in every colour of the rainbow. He planned to wind them up like a huge lollipop and stitch the tubes together to make a floor rug for Nell's birthday. Plan B, in case he didn't make it long enough, was a beanie for Ben.

Perry was knitting a scarf. Nell said that once he'd mastered the art of the scarf, she'd teach him to knit on four needles. Then he could make beanies for boiled breakfast eggs or vests for orphaned lambs. Perry had already decided he wanted to knit mittens for Worzel Gummidge. He felt sorry for the old scarecrow who stood in the vegetable patch all day and all night with his holey coat flapping. Especially in winter, when his straw fingers and carroty nose were covered in frost. A few stitches from Perry's scarf had mysteriously gone astray but Nell said he was doing an excellent job and, anyway, she liked the spiderweb effect the dropped stitches made.

Having Nell compare his scarf to a spider's web was a great compliment to Perry. Both he and Nell loved spiderwebs. She'd shown Perry where to look for them and how to identify which variety of spider had made them. Perry's favourite was Golden Orb. Golden was clever as well as beautiful. Often she spun a web like a fairy's hammock between the veranda posts. By sunrise, her larder would be well stocked with moths and insects that came to feed in the marigolds beside the steps. Early on misty mornings, Perry and Nell would go walking to see the webs on barbed-wire fences sparkling with dewy diamonds, like necklaces fit for the Queen. Perry knew the Queen wore a diamond necklace, because there was a picture of her on Nell's apron and her necklace sparkled when Nell danced the Spanish Fandango. He wondered if they had fence diamonds in England, and if the Queen had ever seen them when she was walking her dogs in the morning.

There was another reason why Perry liked Choose-days. They reminded him of chosen. Chosen is good, Nell says. Chosen is when you get to say yes or no. Before Perry came to the Kingdom of Silk, no one had ever let him choose, not even on Choose-days. They never said the words, they never asked the question. They just telephoned Melody, the welfare lady, and she came and took him back to the children's home after a few weeks. But on the Day of Cake and Thankfulness, Ben said, 'We want you to stay with us, Perry. Is that what you want? Is it? Will you stay with us?'

It was a tender moment and God was in it. Until then Perry thought God was in heaven. Heaven was far away, higher than a cumulonimbus. Perry would never forget Ben's words, because he wanted so much to stay. The Kingdom of Silk was his home now. He had family. He *was* family. He was Saffron's other brother. That's how she introduced him to people he'd never met before.

'And this is Perry, my other brother,' she'd say, holding his hand and smiling at him like it gave her double happiness to have two brothers instead of one.

Suddenly, Perry wanted to be near Saffron because being family and making happy go both ways. He gathered up his knitting and lay down with his head beside hers on Barney's woolly middle. They looked out the open door and watched Golden darning her web and red leaves raining quietly from the Cox's Orange Pippin. They saw the letting go of the last of the wrinkled apples and heard the soft thud of them landing on the tin roof of Annie's white-washed studio.

Perry liked Saffron's quietness. She let him hear things working. Important things, like the tick of the clock - home's heart. A sheep asleep. And magpies gossiping cheerfully about the blueberry sky, the elephant clouds and the sweet green smell of wet in the distance. But there was something else too. Now he had learnt to read hearts, Perry Angel knew Saffron was frightened. So he nestled his hand in hers and, without saying a word, reminded her that a brother's love is real and beautiful, and stronger than fear. It was a tiny tender moment; one that Saffron wanted to write like a bracelet of silver charms across her empty pages.

4. Elephant Clouds and Afternoon Tea

Nell was knitting socks for Jenkins, a matching pair, because Jenkins hadn't been brought up to appreciate oddness. But she noticed the tender moment that happened in the silence between Saffron and her other brother, Perry Angel. She looked at the clock. Its insides still worked but one of the hands was broken. The big one, with the cherub swinging from it, was stuck on half past

the hour. It seemed like the chubby cherub was weighing it down, trying to make time stand still. Nell stood up slowly. The coming wet was already in her bones; it heavied her legs and made the floorboards in the passage creak.

When she reached the door where her favourite poem was painted, Nell stopped. She knew its words by heart but she read them again.

A time to cry and a time to laugh,
A time to be sad and a time to dance …

Nell didn't feel like dancing or laughing, but she didn't exactly feel like crying or being sad either.

She just felt as though she was carrying a heavy load inside herself and could find nothing in the poem that might help lighten it. She sighed, put some water in the kettle, set it on the stove and took the lid off her old brown teapot. Ben would be home soon and they'd share tea and pink jelly cakes and perhaps then the feeling might go away.

While the red leaves rained and Perry held her hand, Saffron rested her Naming Day Book over her heart and breathed in its faint scent of mothballs and musk. She'd read it hundreds of times before, so many times she could almost see it with her eyes shut. But today she wanted to make sure that everything in it was imprinted in her mind so it would be with her even when she was sleeping, even if she was far, far away from the Kingdom of Silk. Even when the fiery halo burned above her brow. And even if she could never see the book again. She dozed until she heard Nell's footsteps in the passageway and the familiar sound of Miss Amelie's tea trolley.

Miss Amelie was a good friend of Nell's. But then she passed away and became a deep mystery, the way she was before she was an egg. There is no need for worldly goods when you become a deep mystery, so Nell bought Miss Amelie's trolley at an auction. She sanded off the layers of dark brown varnish and painted it Captain Blue. The colour reminded her of the small wooden fishing boats on Miss Amelie's postcards from places far away.

Saffron opened her eyes when Nell wheeled the trolley into the room on its wonky casters. Scraps of tablecloth-lace lapped the edges like sea foam, forget-me-not teacups and saucers chattered to

one another and steam spiralled lazily from Brown Betty's cracked spout. There were two tiers on Miss Amelie's tea trolley. On the bottom tier was a small cut-glass dish of sugar-coated aniseed rings, a plate of pink jelly cakes and a tattered copy of *Anne of Green Gables*.

It was Nell's book. She'd had it since she was a young girl and had learnt a lot about being a better person by reading it, even though it was a mostly made-up story. From the moment her daughters were born, Nell read to them. It didn't matter that they didn't understand the words. Books are many things: lullabies for the weary, ointment for the wounded, armour for the fearful and nests for those in need of a home. When Ben came to live with Nell, she read to him too. Sometimes still, she and Ben would sit in the big comfy armchairs in the living room and read alternate chapters to one another. It was a leftover habit from when Ben was a boy. When he grew up and married, he and Nell took turns reading to the Rainbow Girls, Griffin and Layla, and to Perry Angel, who was not an orphan like Anne of Green Gables, but a foster child, like Ben.

Nell was like a library of one book with her *Anne of Green Gables*. She was always loaning it to someone. She loaned it to the preacher once and suggested he read some of it to his congregation. Nell didn't go to church very often, but she and the preacher were good friends. They enjoyed arguing, especially about books and other important things. But they agreed that L. M. Montgomery was a very fine writer, and that God can sometimes be found in a pumpkin patch or the blanketing blue hills and is always present in a tender moment.

After Perry came to stay, Nell loaned her Anne book to Sunday Lee, Perry's birth mother, because she wanted Sunday to understand what a blessing Perry was to the Silks and what an unselfish thing she had done when she was sweet sixteen and couldn't care for her baby boy. Books can do things like that.

Saffron believed in the power of books but, on that particular Tuesday, she tried hard not to worry about what it would be like if you weren't well enough to read. How could you be brave then, how could you be healed, where would the songs come from, how would you find home?

The magpies had all flown away and the cloud elephants had grown gigantic, blocking out the blueberry sky and trumpeting so loudly that Blue hid under Nell's rocking chair. But none of that distracted Perry from what he was thinking. He was wondering if anyone had ever read to Sunday Lee when she was small. If anyone had cuddled her on their lap with a book and told her stories and pointed to the words so they would become like old friends next time she saw them. Sunday was his other mother, the person who had grown him from an egg in the quiet dark inside her. Perry made up his mind that next time Sunday came to visit the Kingdom of Silk, he would read to her. Maybe the words would soothe the sadness she kept inside.

Annie and Ben arrived just as the elephants began squirting fat drops into the sky. Nell poured the tea, then picked up her Anne book and began to read aloud. And Perry Angel felt suddenly happy: because of his plan, and because he was wearing his Cloud Appreciation Society badge and he knew that the elephants in the sky were called cumulonimbi, and because the words Nell was reading were his old friends.

Saffron felt happy too. The deep, delicious happiness that wraps itself around you when everything is safe and familiar. Brown Betty in her rainbow cosy, Miss Amelie's fishing-boat-blue tea trolley, the book of Anne, Nell's voice, Perry's hand, the fat cherub, the tick and the tock, apple-pie days... a tiny voice inside her head interrupted.

'Can such a feeling last forever?' it asked. 'Even after you turn back into a deep mystery, like Miss Amelie and L. M. Montgomery?'

But she, Saffron Silk, was suddenly Joan-of-Arc-brave and everything in the universe seemed to be in its right and proper place.

5. Tools for Truth

At lunchtime that day, Griffin couldn't eat. Every day for a week he meant to tell Layla about Saffron. And every day he put it off. But now he had to tell her because she'd seen Saffron on Apple-Pie Sunday. Everyone had. They saw the way she'd held on to the table and how Nell and Annie had to help her walk to her bedroom. So Griffin told Layla what he knew: about the headaches, the dizziness and feeling ill.

43

'I think it's been happening for a few months now,' he said. 'It usually lasts for about a day and then she's okay again.'

'Has she been eating ice cream?'

'No, I don't think so. At least, she wasn't on Sunday.'

Layla thought for a while. The only time she got a headache was when she'd been eating ice cream too fast. She always got dizzy if she played blind man's buff or when her daddy gave her too many whizzy dizzies in a row. And once, she went on the Octopus ride at the Royal Agricultural Show and felt sick in the stomach and dizzy as well. But Saffron definitely wasn't doing any of those things on Sunday.

'Maybe it's her ears,' Layla said after a few moments. 'My brother got an ear infection once. That made him lose his balance and feel sick. Doctor Larsson gave Patrick pills and it made him better in no time.'

'She's had pills,' said Griffin, 'all kinds of pills, but none of them seem to work very well.'

'She might need glasses,' Layla said. 'Mum used to get headaches before she got her glasses.'

Glasses, maybe that's all it is. Why didn't I think of glasses? Why didn't Nell or Annie? Griffin thought to himself and his heart seemed a little lighter.

'She has to see the doctor this afternoon.'

'He'll probably do eye tests,' said Layla confidently. 'I always ask Doctor Larsson if I can read his eye chart. I can read everything on it. Even the last line. But I wish I could have glasses. And tell Annie to ask him to look in Saffy's ears with that tiny torch he's got. Just in case she's got what Patrick had.'

Griffin wished he was as good at asking questions as Layla. He remembered something Nell had told him when he was only seven years old.

'Questions are tools for discovering truth. They can be used like a sledgehammer to smash things open, or like a candle to lighten the dark.'

For a moment he wished he could climb onto Nell's knee again or step into the circle of Annie's arms and ask all the questions he so badly wanted answers to. Can an ordinary headache make you fall-down-dizzy, throw up, blind you or worse? Would the truth smash their world into tiny pieces

or would their smiles light up the darkness when they told him that a headache is only a headache and has never killed anyone? What was the point of asking when no one knew the answer? Not Layla, not Nell, not Annie and not even Doctor Larsson. Not yet anyway.

Layla moved closer to Griffin. His hair had grown long again and he was twisting it around his finger, a sure sign he was worried.

'Saffy will be all right, Griff,' she said.

'Doctor Larsson said she might have to go to the city for tests if she keeps getting the headaches,' said Griffin.

Layla wondered what could be so wrong with Saffron that Doctor Larsson couldn't fix it but she didn't want to worry Griffin any further.

'Mum says they've got better equipment in the city. And anyway, remember the wish we made up last Christmas? You know, the deep and silent wish we wrote in my journal.' Layla dragged the dog-eared journal out of her school bag, turned it to the right page and showed Griffin. It was a long wish but the most important part was short.

We, Griffin William Silk and Layla Elliott, wish that if anyone has to leave the Kingdom of Silk, it will not be forever.

The fine print on the end explained important things such as Layla, Perry and Blue being included in the wish. Layla studied the words slowly and carefully, as if they were a magic spell and not just a wish. She wondered if there was some rule about wishes that she and Griffin didn't know. Should they have told someone? Was it like when you invent something and have to make it official so no one else can steal your idea? Maybe she should have given it to her mother to take to work. She could have stamped it with a blue stamp and locked it in the safe. She remembered how they'd showed it to Nell. And Nell thought it was a good wish, didn't she? Then she remembered Nell saying something like, 'But none of us can stay here forever, no matter how much we want to.'

Layla hadn't taken much notice then. She knew that when you got as old as Scarlet, you might think about going away to university. But Saffron wasn't old enough to go to university for a long time yet and, even if she was, it wouldn't be forever.

These are the thoughts that came into Layla's head while she and Griffin sat in the playground under the elm tree. It was the worst place to sit on a day like Tuesday because the breeze blew and the leaves jostled against each other and whispered, *Tishkin, Tishkin.*

For half a heartbeat Layla wondered if something really bad was happening to Saffron... something that meant she might never come home. Something like dying.

Griffin sometimes talked to Layla about Tishkin. Usually she enjoyed hearing about his baby sister. But thinking about Tishkin today and hearing the leaves whisper her name when Saffron was ill made Layla feel nervous all over. So she made herself concentrate on reading the fine print. When she had finished, she ate half of Griffin's peanut butter and honey sandwich. It is difficult to swallow when you are nervous all over. But Layla did it to encourage Griffin to eat the other half, because that is what friends are for.

Layla wouldn't hear of Griffin going to the doctor's surgery without her, even though it would mean missing out on her favourite television program. The Elliotts' house was on the way to Doctor Larsson's rooms. Layla's parents were still at work when school finished for the day, so she pinned a note to the door, telling them where she had gone.

6. Sir Attenborough and the Velvet Worms

The wet and the school bus arrived at the Colour Patch Café at the same time. The sky was so dark that Mr Kadri's neon sign had switched itself on. Scarlet, Indigo, Violet and Amber stepped off the bus outside the café, where the footpath was awash with the colours of paradise.

Scarlet wished she had asked her friend Anik to come with her. Anik had learnt what courage meant when he and his family rolled up their belongings in a rug and left everything and everyone they loved to start again in a new land where no one spoke their language, no one understood. Here, in the small town of Cameron's Creek, they had found a scrap of paradise above the Colour Patch Café.

But Scarlet had not asked Anik and he'd gone to his Advanced English class, and now she was worried about what would happen if the doctor wanted to send Saffron to hospital. Hospital was where Doctor Larsson sent patients he couldn't fix. Hospital was where Tishkin went. There was nothing about Tishkin that could be fixed. She was new and perfect in every way except she had stopped breathing. Saffron was different. She wasn't new. She breathed but she hurt. It seemed like something inside her head was wrong. Knowing all this, Scarlet asked herself, how could she or any of her family, possibly have courage? Perhaps Anik could tell her.

When she and her sisters arrived at the surgery, the Bedford was parked outside and Blue and Barney were huddled together under the porch at the top of the five slate steps. Inside, Perry and

Griffin were sitting on the floor, trying to find wooden Mrs Noah in the toy box to help wooden Mr Noah catch the wooden zebras who wouldn't walk up the ramp because they were frightened of the silent roaring of the wooden tigers.

Layla was sitting on a grey plastic chair, pretending to read about raising pigs in a magazine that was four years old and had the cover torn off. But she accidentally started thinking about Tishkin and wondering whether the deep and silent wish in her journal was as powerful as she had thought it was when she and Griffin made it. She tried to smile at the Rainbow Girls, but the nervous-all-over feeling started to come back again, so after a while she pushed open the heavy red door and went outside.

With the hood of her yellow raincoat pulled over her head, Layla walked down the steps to the footpath and waded into the overflowing gutter. Storm water eddied dangerously close to the tops of her gumboots and sideways rain needled her cheeks. She made a seed-pod sailing ship, loaded it with an invisible cargo of nervous-all-over and set it afloat on a voyage to the unknown, gazing after it till it disappeared into a grate in the ground. Then she stomped slowly back up the steps to the cherry door with its peek-a-boo letter slot, dragon knocker and shiny brass nameplate. She pulled a crumpled windcheater from her bag, wiped her face then polished the raindrops off Doctor Larsson's name and all the letters of his learning that followed.

Barney and Blue didn't look any more cheerful than Layla felt. She put the windcheater down on the top step and sat on it. Blue sat beside her, rested his head on her knee and gazed into her eyes. Rain dripped from the eaves into Layla's polka-dot gumboots. She sighed and emptied them into the Michaelmas daisies.

Everyone who knew Layla properly said she was a girl of great determination. Being determinedly cheerful and kind and brave when someone dear to you is ill isn't easy. But Layla loved the Silks more than anyone else in the world, except her own family, so she made up her mind not to let them down. She wrapped her arms around Blue's neck and hugged him.

'Don't worry, Blue,' she said. 'Doctor Larsson's very smart. You can tell by all the letters after his name. He'll do everything he can to make Saffron well again.'

Noah's ark had been loaded, unloaded and loaded again by the time Layla went back inside and someone had drawn black spectacles on the pigs and whiskers on all the people in the magazine she'd been looking at. The Rainbow Girls were watching television. When the commercial break came on, Layla went to the reception desk. She waited while the lady behind the counter shuffled papers. It was a tall counter and Layla was a small girl, so after the hamburger commercial finished, she fetched a plastic chair from the play area, carried it to the desk and stood on it to make sure she could be seen. The lady kept shuffling. She was wearing a badge with her name on it. Layla had plenty of time to read it.

'Excuse me please, Colleen,' she said. 'Have you got the documentary channel on your TV? There's a really good nature show on it.'

'It's flu shot day for seniors and that means there are a lot of other people waiting too, dear,' said Colleen without looking up. 'They mightn't all want to watch your nature show.'

'It's not my show, it's Sir Attenborough's,' said Layla, 'and it's very educational. Today it's about velvet worms, which aren't really worms at all because they grew legs and came out of the sea millions of years ago and now they live in rainforests.'

Colleen looked up then and arranged her orange lips in a straight line, like an elastic band fully stretched. Layla had seen this look before, on her mother's face. It was a warning to stop. But Layla didn't. She said calmly and ever so slightly more loudly, 'And besides, my mother says *The Bored and the Beautiful* is a romantical drama and it isn't suitable viewing for children.'

Colleen frowned and said, 'Does your mother have an appointment, dear?'

'No, she's at work. I'm here with my friends, the Silks. They don't have a television at home, they do interesting stuff instead. But I don't think Annie and Ben and Nell would approve of us watching romantical dramas.'

Mr Fairchild, of Fairchild & Sons Butchery, who didn't have the usual number of fingers on his left hand, was waiting in the corner by the mother-in-law's tongue plant. Suddenly he made a loud spluttering sound, leant forward with his head in his hands and began to shake uncontrollably.

The lady next to him said, 'Heavens above, what's wrong, Alfie?'

Mr Fairchild uttered a strange wheezing sound and the lady leapt from her chair and hurried to the counter.

'Quick, get the doctor,' she said to Colleen. 'I think Mr Fairchild's had an allergic reaction to the mother-in-law plant!'

Colleen stopped fiddling with her papers and rushed out from behind her desk. 'What's the matter, Mr Fairchild? You haven't been eating the plant have you? It's poisonous!'

Mr Fairchild shook his head and fumbled in the pocket of his tweed jacket. Tears streamed down his face.

'Can I fetch you a glass of water? Do you suffer from asthma?'

He pulled out a handkerchief, mopped his eyes, blew his nose, slapped his knee and shook his head. He didn't look the slightest bit ill to Layla. There were smiling lines at the corners of his eyes and his cheeks were two fat buns. Mr Fairchild was laughing!

You can catch things from other people in doctors' waiting rooms. Things like coughs and colds, and sometimes, but not often, laughter. Mr Fairchild's laughter was the highly contagious kind and soon everyone was giggling. At last the butcher drew a deep breath and said, 'For pity's sake, Colleen, would you switch to Sir Attenborough's show? I think I've got an allergy to romantical dramas.'

Layla had heard of people having allergies to things like medicine or eggs or peanut butter, but never, ever to romantical dramas. Mr Fairchild winked at her and she had a distinct feeling it was something she'd done that had made him laugh. She wasn't sure what it was but it didn't matter; she was taking care of her friends and soon they were watching Sir Attenborough with a torch on his head and a beautiful velvet worm crawling over his fingers, and not thinking quite as much about why Saffron's appointment was taking so long.

7. Different Ways of Looking

Saffron had never owned a teddy bear. She had Barney instead. But sheep, even well-behaved ones, were not permitted in the doctor's rooms. Saffron knew from experience that no amount of pleading or waving *'sheep have feelings too'* placards in the waiting room had any effect on Colleen. Last time, Colleen had said, in a shouty sort of voice, 'If I let Barney in, Blue will expect to come in as well! This is a doctor's surgery, Saffron, not a vet's.'

This time, Saffron couldn't be bothered arguing with Colleen, so she came in jeans and her old woolly jumper, which was the next best thing to having Barney in the room.

Just as Layla said, Doctor Larsson had a torch. But it wasn't for shining into ears. It was an ophthalmoscope and the doctor explained it was used for looking into people's eyes. Saffron didn't care what fancy name the doctor gave his torch. She didn't want to know anything about his world of medicine, illness and instruments. Hers was a joyful world of imagination, discovery, books, myths, legends, magic and grandmotherly wiseness. And that was how she wanted it to stay.

She told herself that when Doctor Larsson shone his tiny torch through the windows of her mind he'd see a universe inside. Her universe, and every part of it would be beautiful. There would be colour and movement. The doctor would be amazed. He would see all the stories Saffron had ever read, all the songs she'd sung, the laughter heard, the tears cried, the hands held. All her

tender moments would shimmer there in the dark as brilliantly as the moon and stars she saw when she slept with her brothers and sisters in their tree house.

The tender moment when Mama gave birth to Griffin would be there. And Daddy's tears when he held his first son up to the forget-me-not sky. One for Mama explaining to them all how her love for them, and theirs for her, would help ease the ache of their Tishkin-shaped emptiness. Surely the doctor couldn't miss seeing that moment when a small boy was given a choice for the first time in his life, when Daddy asked Perry Angel if he wanted to become part of their family and stay with them forever and for always at the Kingdom of Silk. And Nell would be there too. Nell was the beginning and the end of every tender moment in Saffron's universe. In the air she breathed.

When Doctor Larsson laid his torch on his desk, Saffron knew immediately that he hadn't seen her tender moments, not even one of them. She knew because it wasn't possible for anyone to look upon such loveliness without it showing in their eyes.

The world is filled with interesting people. Some like wearing matching socks, some prefer odd ones and others never wear socks at all. There are fans of romantic television dramas, and those who prefer to view the secret life of velvet worms. Like Saffron, some have only to close their eyes to see extraordinary things, like memories of tender moments, while others, despite their bright lights, brass nameplates and X-ray machines, cannot.

Doctor Larsson, kind, clever and wishful though he was, did not know how to recognise tender moments. When he shone his tiny torch through the windows of his patients' minds he did not expect to see something that would rival the beauty of the Milky Way, the moon or Mars. So, sadly, he never did. All he ever found were shadowy things that needed further investigation.

Over their many years of living, Nell, Ben and Annie had come to understand that both kinds of people and both ways of looking and believing are important. Especially when someone isn't well.

Doctor Larsson was like a detective looking for clues with his torch and his stethoscope. His job was to question the victim and the witnesses and get to the bottom of the mystery. He asked Saffron, Annie, Ben and Nell all the questions he could think of. How often did Saffron feel unwell? Which part of her head ached? What other symptoms had she experienced? He didn't mention halos or firebirds and Saffron didn't tell him. Doctor Larsson had no reason to believe she was withholding information. He was careful not to name a suspect before he had evidence. Careful not to frighten his patient. Careful as a new father with his baby.

At Saffron's Naming Day Ceremony, the doctor had nodded his head when Ben read the line in his poem about the mystery of Saffron. In his experience, many people think a child ceases to be a mystery once it is born, simply because they can hold it, hear it, see it and smell it. But Doctor Larsson had three daughters of his own, Sonja, Ingrid and Pia, and despite all his knowledge of science and medicine, he still found humans of all ages wonderfully mysterious creatures. Like Ben, he'd once believed that with each passing day his girls would become less of a mystery to him. Now Sonja, Ingrid and Pia were adults with families of their own, yet he still found them as mysterious as ever. He wondered how much Ben and Annie had learnt about Saffron and how much was still a mystery.

At the end of the interview, Doctor Larsson asked if there were any questions. Saffron had many: What's wrong with me? What did you see inside my head? What about the firebirds? Am I mad? Will I go blind? Will I die?

But she didn't ask any of them. She couldn't. Not with the people she loved most there in the room with her. Not after what had happened to Tishkin.

She sat on her hands and stared at the squares in the tartan carpet while Doctor Larsson wrote a letter with a scratchy pen to a person she didn't know. He put it in an envelope, sealed it and wrote a name on the front. Then he gave it to Ben and told him to take Saffron to a hospital in the city, where someone would take photographs of the inside of her head.

8. The Loud Silence of Saffron Silk

Saffron rode home in the cabin of the old Bedford, sandwiched between Annie and Nell. Colleen called a taxi-bus for the rest of the family. If it hadn't been raining, Saffron would have sat in the back of the truck with Blue and Barney. They didn't speak English, they didn't ask questions, but Saffron was certain they understood how she felt.

Nell didn't ask questions either. She said, 'Doctor Larsson's just being careful. He's making sure there's nothing he's not aware of, that's all.' Nell was being careful too.

He doesn't know everything because I didn't tell him everything, Saffron thought, then wondered if she'd made a mistake not mentioning the firebirds. She closed her eyes, soaked up the comforting warmth of her mother and grandmother and tried to guess by the motion of the truck how close they were to home. There was no hammering, no candles, no questions, just the slap of the wipers, the hum of the engine and the crackle of the radio as they drove over potholes and puddles towards the Kingdom of Silk.

Dinner that evening was Saffron's favourite: pumpkin soup with crusty rolls, and apple pie for dessert. But Saffron barely touched hers and asked if she could be excused.

'Stay with us a while,' said Annie, 'even if you don't feel like eating.'

So Saffron stayed. She quietly arranged grains of spilt salt into snail-shaped spirals and checked her fingernails. She did not look at Griffin, taste the sunset-coloured soup, pass the rolls to Scarlet, or smile. Not once, to anyone.

The people who knew Saffron best were used to her long silences and understood there were many reasons for them. Good reasons, like reading about gods and mortals, designing and sewing costumes, imagining life in ages gone by, filling entire rolls of lunch-wrap with fake hieroglyphics or painting leather sandals on her feet with brown boot polish.

Some of her more complicated projects involved many hours of silence. For example, a stage production of *Anne of Green Gables*. Saffron had read the book over and over to make sure she knew it by heart. All the details were in her head. She'd hire the school hall. There would be red carpet to cover the cracked cement path, deep purple curtains to swish open and shut. She wanted footlights and spotlights and flashing bulbs around the billboard like Mr Kefalas had on his fish and chip shop sign. Nell would play Marilla and Mr Jenkins would be Matthew. Scarlet with her dark hair would play Anne's 'bosom friend', Diana. Layla's brother, Patrick, would make a very handsome Gilbert Blythe and she, Saffron, would play the part of Anne. Violet would write the script.

But tonight, Saffron's silence was different. The reason behind it was not good. It was a silence that everyone seemed to notice. It was wide and deep and long and weighed heavily upon their shoulders. It was a loud silence. It shouted.

Perhaps Griffin noticed it more than the others. It squeezed his heart to think of Saffron so full of unasked questions, for there had been a time when he was silent. It began when his baby sister was born. Before that Griffin was the full stop at

the end of the Silk family, the pot of gold at the end of the Rainbow Girls, the icing on the cake. His daddy said so in his Naming Day speech. But then Tishkin came and Griffin was no longer the youngest, no longer special. He was lost somewhere in the middle of his big, busy family. He loved his baby sister and didn't mean to be jealous, but he was. He didn't want her to die, but she did. Griffin was afraid she had read his jealous heart and that hers had broken because of it. He was afraid of what people would think of him if they found out.

So Griffin became silent. He dared not ask if there was something he could have done to prevent Tishkin's death, or why Annie had to stay in a hospital for very sad people and if she would ever come home again. The silence grew, as though it was an infectious disease or an evil enchantment that prevented the Silks from talking about Tishkin at all.

Then, one daisy-filled day, Griffin met Layla, Queen of Hearts, and the spell was broken. Ben used to say that Layla had been sent to comfort them after Tishkin went away. He said she was like an arm around their shoulders, a candle in the dark. And it was true. Layla shone so brightly that there was no room inside Griffin for fear to hide. Like a true friend she comforted him, made him feel he wasn't alone and helped him discover it was normal to feel guilty even though he wasn't.

Tonight, Griffin watched Annie trying to include Saffron in the conversation and saw how stubbornly his sister stayed silent. She was making Annie sad, making them *all* sad, not looking at their faces, not seeing their hurt or their love. She had shut herself away from them in a tower of silence. Every kindness bounced off the high stone walls of her imaginary castle. Something had to be done about Saffron.

Griffin was a thoughtful child who enjoyed the company of animals. A patient person who would wait quietly for hours to glimpse an eagle soar above the hills, a kind boy who saved snails from certain death in Nell's vegetable patch and re-housed them in rushes near the dam. Griffin was definitely not a loud person. But he hated what Saffron's silence was doing to them all. His hate and rage quickly grew so powerful that he couldn't sit at the table a moment longer. He sprang to his feet. His fist came down like a sledgehammer beside his soup bowl. His chair toppled backwards and crashed loudly onto the wooden floor and he shouted into the shocked silence, 'You're not being fair, Saffron! We're worried too, but it's not fair what you're doing to us. You won't let us be kind. Tell her, Nell, tell her it's not fair to shut us out!'

As Griffin ran towards the door, Nell opened her arms like wings and gathered him in against the Queen's diamonds.

'Tell her what you told me. Tell her about the silence and the candle and the sledgehammer. Please, Nell!' He buried his face in her apron and sobbed.

Saffron had never wondered how much her brother loved her. She was old enough to know that love is elastic, that there is always enough to go around, to hold families together. She had never bothered to ask herself, how wide, how deep, how strong. Knowing it existed was enough for her. But that evening she learnt something else about love. It can transform people. Love had made a lion of Griffin. It gave him courage and made him roar.

9. Saint Lucy's Cats

Doctor Larsson didn't usually make house calls. His only exceptions were when they involved matters of the heart or a member of the Silk family. On this occasion it was both.

He put his favourite jumper on. The cobalt blue one with cables down the front that Hilde knitted when they first became sweethearts. The frayed cuffs had been darned to keep them from completely unravelling and Charlie's dog hair wouldn't come out no matter how many times it was washed. He'd nursed Charlie in it when he was old and dying. The dog was buried under the silver birch where the clump of pink nerines grew. Doctor Larsson didn't mind the mends or the hairs: they brought back treasured memories.

The doctor grew up in a house with seven bedrooms, a grand piano, a crystal chandelier, a fountain in the front garden and roast beef every Sunday. He had everything he needed; everything except tender moments. He knew Nell Silk specialised in tender moments and was sure she would approve of a jumper like his. He was pleased she'd telephoned. A doctor can only do and say so much at an appointment. There is no time for stories. Doctor Larsson kissed Hilde, who had been his wife for fifty-three years now, and told her not to wait up for him. He stepped into his gumboots, checked his pocket for the recipe and rehearsed the story of Lussekatter all the way to the Kingdom of Silk.

Barney and Blue were huddled together on the red vinyl couch when the doctor arrived. They watched him read the note pinned to the veranda post, warning him to avoid Golden Orb's masterpiece. The front door was open. He stepped inside, paused to read the poem painted there, then walked slowly down the passageway, admiring the portraits Annie had painted of her children. Above him, a flock of paper birds wheeled and a galaxy of tart-tin stars cascaded like a spangled chandelier.

The doctor was almost seventy-three and he wondered, as he walked beneath the stars, if age was the reason for the feeling. He'd noticed that it came to him whenever he visited the Kingdom of Silk or when he put his cobalt blue jumper on or when Hilde held his hand as they went walking. Simple things.

The aroma of sunset soup mingling with notes from Ben's harmonica beckoned Doctor Larsson to the kitchen. But suddenly he stopped and turned to look again at the stars, the birds, the portraits and the poem. At that moment he understood what they all were, what they meant, why they made him feel the way he did. The contents of

the house were a collection of tender moments lovingly gathered by its occupants.

After Doctor Larsson had sampled Nell's sunset soup he began to tell the story he'd carried in his head and his heart for many years. Tonight would be the first time he had told it to anyone other than his own family.

'My youngest daughter's name is Pia,' he began, 'and when she was five years old, we discovered she had a disease. There was treatment, but it involved many, many visits to the hospital and no one could say for sure if it would cure her.

'Sometimes she had to stay there for days or weeks. Sometimes it seemed like the treatment was worse than the illness. Pia begged us not to take her back to the hospital, and Hilde and I wondered if we were doing the right thing.

'Often we would read to Pia, sometimes almost all the night. We found this was one of the few things that stopped her thinking about her illness and the treatment. A couple of weeks before Christmas, in the year Pia turned six, she was back in hospital. Christmas in Sweden is a dark, cold time of the year. One evening, as we sat by Pia's bed, I heard singing. I thought it might have been carolers, so I went to the window. The street lights were on and snow was falling, but I couldn't see anyone. After a while, the singing seemed to be getting closer. So I went to the door of the ward and looked through the glass. The corridor was long and the lights were dim so the patients could sleep but, at the end of it, I saw flickering yellow lights, like a halo of fire, moving slowly towards the children's ward.'

Saffron had been enjoying Doctor Larsson's story and trying to imagine what it would be like to celebrate Christmas in winter. But she was shocked when he mentioned the lights. They sounded so like her firebirds that she wondered if he had known about them all along. Perhaps other people could see them too. The doctor continued his story.

'As they came closer I could see a girl wearing a long white dress. On her head was an evergreen wreath lit by lights that looked like candles. She and the other singers came and stood by Pia's bed where we could see them clearly. All the girls wore white dresses and red sashes and the boys wore cone-shaped hats decorated with gold stars.

'I'd been so worried about Pia that I'd forgotten what day it was. In Sweden, it's traditional to celebrate Saint Lucy's Day on the thirteenth of December, which is about the time of the longest night of the year in the northern hemisphere. We celebrate the end of darkness and new beginnings with street processions, lights and bonfires.

'Stories about Saint Lucy and her good deeds have been told in Sweden for hundreds of years. One of the loveliest, often told to children, is that Lucy would secretly visit people who were forced to hide in caves under the city of Rome because of what they believed. Lucy would come to them at night, wearing candles on her head to light the way so her hands were free to carry food. Lucy means "light", so it was a very good name for her.'

Saffron tried to imagine living in a cave because of your beliefs and how wonderful it would be to see the golden halo coming towards you through the dark.

Doctor Larsson was enjoying telling his story of Pia and Saint Lucy. Saffron, with her eyes big and bright, reminded him of Pia all those years ago: listening, watching, imagining and forgetting for a while what was happening to her.

'Before the children moved further on into the ward, they gave Pia some Lussekatter to eat next morning. Lussekatter means Lucy's Cats,' explained Doctor Larsson. 'They're special buns flavoured with saffron and shaped like curled-up cats. Pia went to sleep holding her Lussekatter.

'It wasn't the last time she had to stay in hospital, but from that night onwards she never seemed to get as upset as she once had. Eventually she got well again. Many years later, she told us that every time she had treatment Saint Lucy would come to her, walking through the dark with candles in her hair and Lussekatter in her hands. She would stop by Pia's bed and tell her that the longest night was almost over.'

Silence fell again at the Kingdom of Silk.

At last Nell found her voice. 'Thank you, Doctor Larsson,' she said. 'That was a beautiful story.'

The doctor fished in his pocket then and pulled out a folded piece of paper.

'Hilde made the best Lussekatter in all Sweden and now in Australia she still makes them for our girls and their children. She wrote out the recipe in case you'd like to make some.'

When the doctor arrived home, his wife was in bed. But she opened her eyes and watched him carefully fold his cobalt blue jumper. As they lay in bed he told Hilde about Golden Orb, about Blue and Barney, about the poem on the open door, the portraits on the wall, the paper birds and the tart-tin stars. He told her how he'd shared sunset soup, Pia's story and afterwards a seat on the old red couch. There wasn't much room for them all: Blue and Barney, Annie, Nell, Saffron and the doctor. Ben sat on the veranda boards softly playing a lilting love song to the moon while Saffron told them about the firebirds.

Hilde Larsson smiled and held her doctor's hand until they went to sleep.

10. Farewell to Little Petal

Saffron was leaving on the 6:00pm train on Sunday. Her photographs would be taken on Monday. Nobody really knew what would happen after that.

On Wednesday morning, before she left for school, she made her family promise that, until the moment she stepped on the train, everything would go on as usual at the Kingdom of Silk. Of course they agreed, but that didn't stop each of them wanting to do something special for her.

Even Scarlet was making an effort. She hadn't been able to think of anything useful that she could do well. Amber could cook, Violet could write and Indigo could paint and draw. According to Violet, Scarlet was *flamboyantly* untidy. Scarlet secretly consulted the dictionary where 'flamboyant' was defined as 'having a very showy or colourful appearance', a fairly accurate description of the state of her bedroom. But flamboyance isn't all that useful when you want to do something nice for your youngest sister. The simplest thing seemed to be to ask Saffron what she would like.

Saffron didn't hesitate. 'Could you look after Barney and be especially nice to him in case he misses me?' she asked. She almost mentioned adoption, just in case, but decided not to.

Scarlet promised faithfully that she would and immediately decided to ask Mr Kadri if she could take Barney to work with her on Sunday.

Layla was waiting at the school gate when Griffin arrived. She wanted to know what Doctor Larsson had told them about Saffron's dizziness and headaches.

'She does have to go to hospital for tests,' Griffin said.

'Did he say what he thinks is the matter?'

'Not really. He said headaches can sometimes make people feel dizzy and sick. But he wants to get photographs of the inside of her head to make sure there's nothing that shouldn't be there.'

'Is Saffron all right?'

'I think so. She's gone back to school today. But that's what usually happens. She gets the headache and the dizzy spells and feels sick. Then if she lies down in the dark for about a day, she's normal again.'

'Is she scared about the tests?'

'I didn't ask her. But Doctor Larsson came to our house last night. He told us a story from when his daughter Pia was in hospital. Afterwards, Saffron went and sat on the veranda with the doctor, and Nell said she talked to him about things she didn't say at the appointment.'

The bell for going inside rang then, but at break time Layla asked Griffin to tell her Pia's story.

'Oh Griff, it's beautiful!' said Layla when he'd finished. 'It makes me feel kind of peaceful inside. Do you think that's how Saffron felt when she heard it?'

'I hope so,' Griffin said.

Time seemed to pass at twice the speed of light that week and suddenly it was Sunday. Everyone at the Kingdom of Silk was busy trying to keep their promise to Saffron, to be as normal as possible. It seemed harder at weekends when they were all at home.

Scarlet left for work half an hour early because Barney didn't understand about punctuality. He strolled and she let him on account of her promise to Saffron. Mr Kadri agreed to allow Barney to come to the Colour Patch Café as long as he didn't come inside. Mr Kadri had a soft spot for Saffron. He was born in a country where the fields were covered in crocus flowers, the plant from which a spice called saffron is harvested. He called her Little Petal, and it made him sorry inside to know she wasn't well.

When Scarlet and Barney arrived, Mr Kadri made a chocolate-flavoured milkshake with an extra scoop of ice-cream. He served it in a soup bowl because Barney wasn't used to drinking through a straw and his nose wouldn't fit inside a paper cup. Afterwards, Mr Kadri's curly-haired children wiped Barney's milky chin with paper napkins. Then they led him to the courtyard and drew crayon portraits of him on butcher's paper and sang sheepish songs to him.

At lunchtime, some visitors to Cameron's Creek arrived at the Colour Patch Café. When Mr Kadri brought them their mint tea, they enquired if it was common in the country to see a sheep asleep under a bus stop seat.

'No, no, not at all common,' said Mr Kadri. 'But, you see, Barney is the black sheep of Little Petal, who is the sister of Miss Crimson, who is the daughter of Mr Benjamin Silk and his lovely wife with all the many children and the grandmother. Little Petal is going to the city to have her photograph taken and we are taking very good care of Barney until she is returning to us.'

While Scarlet and Barney were at work, Annie and Indigo rode their bicycles to Lake Tom Thumb to sketch the sacred ibises. Indigo loved drawing these graceful fishing birds, but often got the letters of their name mixed up and wrote *scared* ibises, instead. Once, when Violet pointed out her mistake, Indigo said, 'We can't all be good at spelling, and anyway, I think I might be ambidextrous.'

Violet explained that ambidextrous meant you could use either hand equally well.

'Perhaps you mean dyslexic,' she suggested kindly. Violet was almost always polite, even to her very loud twin sister. 'That's when your brain doesn't...'

'That's not what I meant!' said Indigo shoutily, realising her mistake. 'I'm trying to improve my drawing by using my left hand. And anyway, the birds all fly away when we set up our easels, so we have to disguise ourselves as bushes till they come back, and I can tell you, it's not very comfortable. So they *are* scared ibises, Miss Smarty Pants!'

On Sunday, Annie and Indigo didn't really care if they saw any ibises at all, scared *or* sacred. Neither of them told the other but each of them knew. Which proves it is possible for very loud, ambidextrous people to have the gift of reading hearts. So instead, Annie painted a picture of Indigo painting a pelican.

While they were gone, Amber was in the kitchen baking. She almost always baked something for afternoon tea on weekends. But today she was making something she'd never made before. She would like to have practised at least once before Saffron went away, but the ingredients cost almost a full week's pay from her newspaper delivery round so she couldn't afford to.

Perry Angel wanted to give something precious to Saffron. The most precious things he could think of were fence diamonds. But you cannot keep a dewdrop-diamond necklace forever or even until lunchtime, because dewdrops fall when the sun shines or the wind blows. So Perry began to think about things that helped him feel brave when he was frightened. Blue was his best thing. He had only to touch Blue's warm freckled back or his triangle ears and he felt better. But he didn't think Blue would be allowed in the hospital. Other than Blue, who wasn't really Perry's to give, and fence diamonds, which belong to everyone, Perry owned two precious things. He wished it was Choose-day so he could make up his mind which one to give his sister. Then he decided to give them both to Saffron. Double happiness from her other brother.

In small towns like Cameron's Creek, news travels fast. At 5:45pm, Mr Kadri hung the closed sign on the door of the Colour Patch Café and took his wife and children to the station to wave goodbye to Little Petal. Scarlet and Anik went too, leading Barney on a pink plastic skipping rope. At five minutes to six, the small platform was almost filled with people who had come to wish Saffron goodbye. Doctor Larsson was there and Elsie-from-the-post-office, Anik's grandma Mosas, Layla's parents and her brother, Patrick. Miss Cherry came too, with her small scruffy dog.

Anik was holding Scarlet's hand and Perry was holding Nell's and wishing Jenkins would hold her other one, because hands have a special language

of their own that you can use when you can't find
the right words to say. He touched Blue to get
the power and felt it surge up his arm. There was
just enough of it to keep him from crying when
the train pulled out of the station, taking Ben and
Annie and Saffron away. He hoped his sister would
be pleased with her double happiness when she
unpacked at the hospital.

11. Double Happiness

Ben's luggage had gone missing. The railway people in the city said it was still at Cameron's Creek and promised to deliver it first thing the next day. A taxi took Annie, Ben and Saffron to a hotel near the hospital. Saffron's appointment was at nine o'clock the following morning.

While Annie and Ben tried to sleep, Saffron jotted her thoughts down on a creamy page of hotel stationery:

LOST!
luggage
and us lost
without it
nothing from home
to hold on to
nothing to comfort us.

A space shuttle
with invisible walls
rocketed
fifteen floors up
higher than a fairytale castle
almost to the moon
too high
for escaping
too high
for a prince to climb
or call
Rapunzel, Rapunzel, let down your long hair
no balcony
no Romeo
no way out

fake windows
no cobwebs in corners
no spiders on sills
no bird songs
floating in
no lace curtains
dancing out

emptiness is very neat
tidy space is hard to fill
with words
in strange square places

all night lights
neon girls
skipping over and over
roofs and roads
all night
traffic
with wheels
or feet
or rails
rumbling

no quiet sounds
no sisters snoring
no ticks
no tocks
no squeaking, sagging springs
no old, broken, chipped, familiar, precious objects
no stories on shelves
portraits on walls
creatures on couches
poems on doors
tender moments
no Nell

In the morning, a railway man came to the door with lost luggage, apologies, a smile and a family voucher to the aquarium. Ben walked to the lift with the kind railway man, who opened his wallet and showed Ben a photograph of a little boy. They stepped into the lift, the odd-job man from the country and the railway man from the city, and rode to the roof, where they talked about children and journeys and lost things. When they finished, Ben's eyes were washed and wet, like the sky after rain. The two men shook hands like friends not like the strangers they had been.

When Ben came back into the room, Annie looked at his face. He smiled and held her close. Saffron added a line to her list:

Tender moments can be found in the most surprising places.

Ben unzipped his duffle bag. Clean clothes and books spilt out. Underneath everything else he found what he was looking for and handed it to Saffron.

It was a small and shabby suitcase. The corners

were scuffed, the leather handle worn smooth, the stitching frayed and the five golden letters embossed on its lid were faded. Saffron sat on the bed, nursed the battered case on her knees and slowly traced its letters with her fingers.

It belonged to her other brother. The suitcase in which he'd been abandoned. The people at the welfare home had invented a name to match the letters.

Annie sat down and put her arm around Saffron's shoulders. 'There's something inside it too,' she said, quiet as a page turning.

Saffron pushed the rusty latches sideways and opened the lid. Inside was an egg carved from olive wood.

Perry Angel was the last to finish eating breakfast at the Kingdom of Silk. Soft-boiled egg with ten toast soldiers for dipping in the golden pond. Then it was his turn to help Nell with the dishes. He liked washing the dishes. It meant he got to wear the green dishwashing gloves with the red fingernails, and stand on the chair with the kangaroos carved on the back and make soapsud clouds with the fairy's mop. But this morning he didn't make many clouds and he kept forgetting to mop the plates and cups because he was thinking about Saffron. He wondered if she had got the double happiness yet and if she understood why he'd given them to her.

The suitcase was important to Perry. For a long time it was his only connection to his birth mother, Sunday Lee. Although she couldn't keep him, she cared enough to want him to be safe. Maybe she hoped he would hold on to the one thing she had given him whenever he felt sad or afraid or alone. Perhaps she hoped he would take it with him on his long journey to find a home. The suitcase had done its job now. Perry had found

the Silks, who offered him a home forever and for always. A family who loved him enough to locate the girl who left him in the suitcase and bring them together again.

When Perry read Saffron's heart and knew she was afraid, he'd pulled the suitcase out from under his bed. He was much braver now and had learnt things he didn't know before. He knew that being family and making happy go both ways. So he gave Saffron his suitcase and the wooden egg Ben had given him. Ben saw the egg in a broken olive tree and carved until he set it free. The preacher said the olive tree meant peace. Peace is what happens when someone loves you enough to give you a wooden egg to have and to hold.

Saffron cried. Perry had given her his two most precious possessions. Something to help her find home and something to hold when she needed to be peaceful.

Perry's gifts were not the only ones Ben brought with him from the Kingdom of Silk. There was a paper-thin parcel wrapped in green tissue. Inside was a CD and a folded note that said, 'To be given to the radiologist before testing commences.'

The note wasn't signed. It could have been instructions from Doctor Larsson. But Saffron recognised the handwriting. It was Nell's.

'What's on it?' asked Saffron.

'We haven't listened to it,' said Annie, 'but Nell said you'll understand when you hear it.'

Indigo sent a necklace of tiny paper cranes made from her pelican painting and threaded on blue embroidery silk.

Violet had made a miniature book. The pages were used postage stamps with short messages written on the backs of them, like old-fashioned telegrams or holiday postcards: 'Missing you. Wish you were here. Have started the play. Patrick Elliott says hello. This stamp is from Paris. Elsie-from-the-post-office gave it to me.'

Amber's gift was wrapped in a tea towel. Three curled-up kittens. Lussekatter, made to the doctor's wife's recipe. They looked and smelt delicious but Saffron, Annie and Ben decided to save them until after the tests.

Saffron sat on the bed with the wooden egg in her hand and the other gifts scattered around her. She thought of Griffin's anger and the love that made him roar. Loud, impatient Indigo, carefully folding birds, on the wings of each one a reminder of home; clear blue water, pelican plumes. Violet with a magnifying glass writing telegram messages on tiny pages. Amber spending her paper-run money on ingredients and her time on cooking. Scarlet babysitting Barney Blacksheep at the Colour Patch Café. Before the taxi came to take them to the hospital, Saffron added another line to her jottings:

Love is real and it is everywhere.

12. Science and Technology
vs Tender Moments

On the day of her return to the Kingdom of Silk, Saffron told her family everything, just as Griffin and Nell had wanted her to before she went away. She read the words she'd written at the hotel. Gave her family souvenirs: small soaps and shampoos; biscuits, tea and coffee in tiny packets; and hotel stationery. She showed them the aquarium voucher and talked about the MRI machine, explaining that the letters stood for magnetic resonance imaging and describing what had happened to her.

'I lay on a small flat bed. The radiologist put a thing like a cage over my face, then he pressed a button and the bed slid into the tunnel part of the machine where the photos get taken. It's very loud in there but they can play music to help block out the sound.'

She smiled, remembering what she listened to through the earphones. Fifty minutes and hundreds of images of her brain later, the radiologist stopped the machine and helped her off the bed.

Afterwards, Ben and Annie offered to take Saffron to the aquarium, but all she wanted was to go home to the Kingdom of Silk. They ate Amber's Lussekatter on the way home, saving the raisin eyes till last, licking their sticky fingers.

In the southern hemisphere, the longest night of the year falls in June. But the eighteenth of May, two days after Saffron came home, was the longest, deepest, darkest night of the year at the Kingdom of Silk. Worry and wishfulness swirled like sleet while the Silks waited for morning. Wishful that morning would come soon or that Saint Lucy might come with candles to lighten the darkness. Waiting to hear the telephone ring. Waiting for the results of the MRI scan. Worried about what it might show.

The telephone rang at seven o'clock the following morning. Annie had just finished milking the goats. While she put the milk in the refrigerator, Nell picked up the receiver.

'Good morning,' she said, then put her hand over the mouthpiece and handed it to Annie. 'It's Doctor Larsson.' Her heart thudded under her primrose cardigan.

Doctor Larsson would have made another house call to the Kingdom of Silk except he needed a special light to show the images of Saffron's brain. So he sent the taxi-bus to fetch the Silks to his surgery. He opened the cherry door himself.

It was too early for Colleen. All the Silks had come. It was Saffron's wish. Perry Angel in his pyjamas, the hems of the trousers still damp from his search for fence diamonds. Layla was there, too. She had stayed overnight even though it was a school day.

'Real friends love each other in good times and in bad, Mum,' she reminded her mother. Mrs Elliott couldn't argue with that and wished she'd had a friend like Layla when she was growing up.

Mr Elliott said, 'Even the Silks need the angels on their side at a time like this.'

So Layla packed the wings Nell had made for her and put them on in the morning when the taxi-bus came.

Saffron was wearing her Barney Blacksheep jumper over her nighty and holding the olive-wood egg in her hand. Nell had a dribble of pancake batter on the sleeve of her primrose cardigan. Annie still had her milking overalls and gumboots on and was holding hands with Ben, who had sawdust in his whiskers. But none of that mattered, nothing did, other than being there, squeezed in, packed tight, together.

'Saffron Silk,' said Doctor Larsson gently, 'everything inside your head is as perfect as on the outside.'

He illuminated the images of Saffron's healthy brain.

'The dizziness, feeling sick, blurred vision and even the lights you call firebirds are all symptoms of a type of headache called a migraine. A migraine won't kill you and there are many things we can do to treat the condition.'

The darkest night was over.

The doctor suggested Saffron keep a diary so they could track any foods or activities or other things that might be responsible for starting the migraines. Then he handed her an envelope.

'You left it at the hospital,' he said. 'The radiologist sent it back with the MRI images.'

'Oh thank you,' said Saffron looking inside. 'It's Nell's recording.'

Doctor Larsson looked puzzled. 'The staff at the hospital were impressed by how calm you were,' he said. 'Fifty minutes is a long time for anyone to lie still in an MRI scanner. Some people, even adults, get quite upset by the noise it makes. Others say they feel trapped by the cage or frightened of being in small spaces, like the tunnel. Sometimes we have to stop the machine and bring them out before we've finished. We even have to put some people to sleep before they go into the machine. Was there anything... you didn't...' Doctor Larsson seemed to be having trouble saying what he meant.

He continued, 'This might seem a strange question, but you didn't see anything... you didn't see Saint Lucy, like Pia, did you?'

'No,' said Saffron, 'it isn't strange at all, but I didn't see Saint Lucy.'

Doctor Larsson sighed and his shoulders drooped as though he was disappointed. Then he turned to Nell. 'I must confess, Nell, that I once overheard a comment you made and I've started to wonder if I'm missing something.'

'What was it I said?' asked Nell.

'It was something like, "There are some things science and technology can't explain; miracles are one of them and love is another." At the time I didn't think too much about it, but I've been thinking about Pia's story and wondering if there are others like it.'

'And you thought Saffron might be able to help you?'

'It was just a thought. The staff at the hospital say Saffron had no sedative, no music, but she was absolutely calm for the full fifty minutes. I thought, just for a moment...'

Saffron interrupted.

'I didn't have medicine or music,' she said, 'but I had Nell. You see Nell told me a long time ago that she writes her tender moments down. So I decided to do the same. When the headaches started, I thought I might be going mad like the Maid of Orleans, or blind and I wouldn't be able to read anymore. So I tried to learn my tender moments by heart, but I kept forgetting some. I didn't know about Nell's recording. I just gave the CD to the nurse, she put the headphones on me and I got such a surprise. The whole time I was in the scanner I was listening to Nell remind me of our tender moments. That's why I wasn't scared. I'm never scared when Nell is with me.'

Doctor Larsson thanked Saffron very much for her explanation and said she had helped him more than she would ever know.

He didn't mention that Nell's disc was faulty and the radiologist hadn't used it or that he'd tried to play it himself to make absolutely sure. The Silks would only have told him that there are some things science and technology can't explain. Like love, miracles and tender moments. And this time the doctor thought he might have to agree.

13. An Invitation

The following week, flyers started appearing around the small town of Cameron's Creek. There was one in the window of the Colour Patch Café, another on the noticeboard at Doctor Larsson's surgery; Elsie-from-the-post-office had one on her counter next to the parcel string; the preacher put one in the church newsletter and a copy was mailed to the lost property department of the railways. It was an invitation. This is what it said:

You are invited to celebrate the end
of the longest night.

When: The last Sunday in May

Time: Just before sunrise

Where: The Kingdom of Silk

Dress: Ladies — White dresses with
red sashes

Gents — Hats like upside-down ice-cream
cones with golden stars

Breakfast: Provided courtesy of
Hilde Larsson and Amber Silk

BYO candles

Hilde Larsson's Lussekatter

Saffron is the world's costliest spice. A little goes a long way, but to make the most of the flavour, Hilde warms hers in the oven before using. This recipe makes 24 Lussekatter.

0.5 gram saffron threads

150 grams caster sugar

150 grams butter, melted

300 ml milk

2 packets (14 grams) dried yeast

1 egg, lightly beaten

700 grams plain flour

a pinch of salt

melted butter, extra, for greasing

24 raisins

1 egg, extra, lightly beaten, for glazing

Pre-heat the oven to 250°C.

Place the saffron threads on a piece of aluminium foil and fold to enclose. Place the saffron packet in the oven and set the timer for 30 seconds.

When the timer rings, turn the oven off and remove the saffron packet. Carefully empty its contents into a mortar and pestle. Add a little of the sugar and grind the saffron to a powder.

In a small mixing bowl, combine the ground saffron mixture and the melted butter and set aside to infuse for about half an hour.

In the meantime, gently warm the milk in a small saucepan over low heat until it reaches 37°C. You can test the temperature with a kitchen thermometer. Take care to heat the milk to the right temperature, because if it's too hot it will kill the yeast and your dough will not rise. If it's too cold the yeast might not activate.

Pour the milk into a large mixing bowl then add the yeast and the remaining sugar. Stir until the yeast and sugar dissolve. Add the egg and the saffron-infused butter to the milk mixture and stir to combine. Sift the flour and the salt over the wet ingredients and mix well until the dough comes away from the side of the bowl. Hilde then likes to tip the dough out onto her lightly floured kitchen table and use her hands to knead the dough until it is smooth.

Grease a large clean mixing bowl with the extra melted butter and transfer the dough to the bowl. Cover with a clean tea towel and set aside in a warm place for the yeast to do its work.

After about 30 minutes, turn the dough out onto the table and knead it again. Then divide the dough into 24 equal pieces and roll each piece into a sausage shape about 15–20 cm long. Shape each piece into a figure eight, joining the two ends underneath. Press a raisin into the centre of one end of each of the Lussekatter.

Place the Lussekatter on baking trays lined with non-stick baking paper, cover them with clean tea towels and set aside in a warm place for 90 minutes or until they double in size.

While the Lussekatter are resting, turn the oven back on and pre-heat to 250°C. Just before you bake the Lussekatter, use a pastry brush to glaze them with the extra egg.

Bake for about 15 minutes or until golden brown.

The Tender Moments of Saffron Silk

ISBN: 978-1-907912-32-0

First published in Australia in 2012 by ABC Books for the
Australian Broadcasting Corporation.

This edition first published in the UK by Phoenix Yard Books
Ltd, 2015. Published by arrangement with Rights People, London.

Phoenix Yard Books
Phoenix Yard
65 King's Cross Road
London WC1X 9LW

1 3 5 7 9 10 8 6 4 2

A catalogue record for this book is available from the British
Libray.

www.phoenixyardbooks.com

Also by Glenda Millard

Picture books:
Unplugged!
Bones Maloney and the Raspberry Spiders
Heart of the Tiger
Kaito's Cloth
Mbobo Tree
And Red Galoshes
Angel Breath
Mrs Wiggins' Wartymelons
Applesauce and the Christmas Miracle
For All Creatures
Isabella's Garden
Lightning Jack

Books for younger readers:
When the Angels Came

Fiction for teenagers:
A Small Free Kiss in the Dark
Bringing Reuben Home
The Novice

Collect the series:

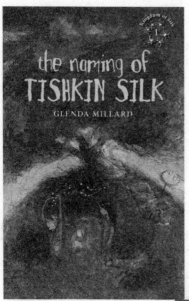

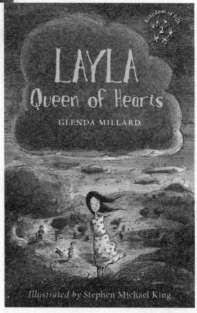

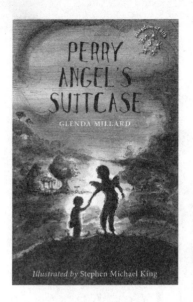

PERRY ANGEL'S SUITCASE

GLENDA MILLARD

Illustrated by Stephen Michael King

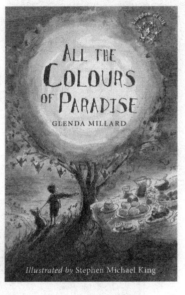

ALL THE COLOURS OF PARADISE

GLENDA MILLARD

Illustrated by Stephen Michael King

PLUM PUDDINGS AND PAPER MOONS

GLENDA MILLARD

Illustrated by Stephen Michael King

Coming soon:

Nell's Festival of Crisp Winter Glories

GLENDA MILLARD

Illustrated by Stephen Michael King